Meet the Author
www.darylcobb.com

D children. Daryl's writing began in college as a Theatre Arts major at Virginia Commonwealth University. He found a freshman writing class inspiring and, combined with his love for music and the guitar, he discovered a passion for songwriting. This talent would motivate him for years to come and the rhythm he created with his music also found its way into the bedtime stories he later created for his children. The story "Boy on the Hill," about a boy who turns the clouds into animals, was his first bedtime story/song and was inspired by his son and an infatuation with the shapes of clouds. Through the years his son and daughter have inspired so much of his work, including "Daniel Dinosaur" and "Daddy Did I Ever Say? I Love You, Love You, Every Day."

Daryl spends a lot of his time these days visiting schools promoting literacy with his interactive educational assemblies "Teaching Through Creative Arts: A Writer's Journey." These performance programs teach children about the writing and creative process and allow Daryl to do what he feels is most important -- inspire children to read and write. He also performs at benefits and libraries with his "Music & Storytime" shows.

Meet the Illustrator
www.illustration-art.net

Other books by Daryl K. Cobb:

"Do Pirates Go To School?"

"Pirates: Legend of the Snarlyfeet"

"Bill the Bat Baby Sits Bella"

"Bill the Bat Finds His Way Home"

"Bill the Bat Loves Halloween"

"Barnyard Buddies: Perry Parrot Finds a Purpose"

"Daddy Did I Ever Say? I Love You, Love You, Every Day"

"Daniel Dinosaur"

"Boy on the Hill"

"Henry Hare's Floppy Socks"

Find all of Daryl's books at www.darylcobb.com

Printed in the USA
Published by 10 To 2 Children's Books

Count With Daniel Dinosaur

Written by Daryl K. Cobb

Illustrated by Carla Castagno

10 To 2 Children's Books / Clinton

No part of this publication may be reproduced, in whole or in part,
without written permission of the publisher.
For information regarding permission, write to:
Ten To Two Children's Books LLC, Attention: Permissions Department,
PO Box 5173, Clinton, N.J. 08809

Text copyright © 2006 by Daryl K. Cobb
Illustrations copyright © 2007 by Carla F. Castagno
All rights reserved. Published by Ten To Two Children's Books LLC.
"Count With Daniel Dinosaur" copyrights and character designs are used under
license from Daryl K. Cobb & Carla F. Castagno by Ten To Two Children's Books LLC.
Book design by Daryl Cobb, Manuela Pentangelo and Carla F. Castagno.
10 To 2 Children's Book logo was created by Manuela Pentangelo.
10 To 2 Children's Books and associated logo are trademarks of Ten To Two Children's Books LLC.
10 To 2 Children's Books logo characters and names are trademarks of Daryl K. Cobb
and are used under license by Ten To Two Children's Books LLC.

ISBN 9781453793763

Written by Daryl K. Cobb
Illustrated by Carla F. Castagno

10to2childrensbooks.com

First Printing 2008

To my family – CC, KC and JC – who I can always count on for inspiration.

Daryl K. Cobb

I dedicate all my pictures to my son, Andrea and especially to my husband, Roberto.

Carla Castagno

Count a little, count some more, count with Daniel Dinosaur.

1 One me

3 Three chairs

Bread goes very well with stew.
I will have a slice or two.

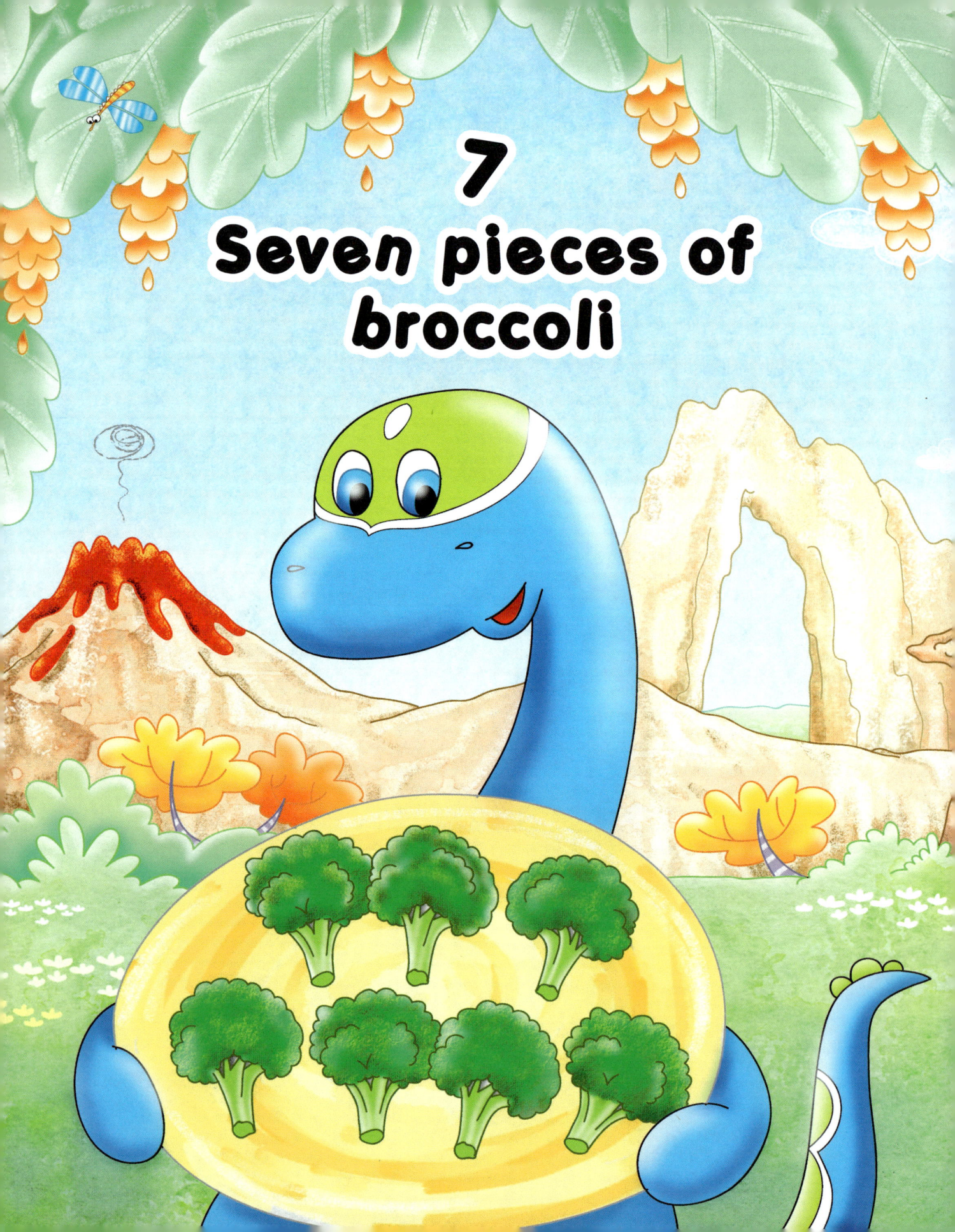

7
Seven pieces of broccoli

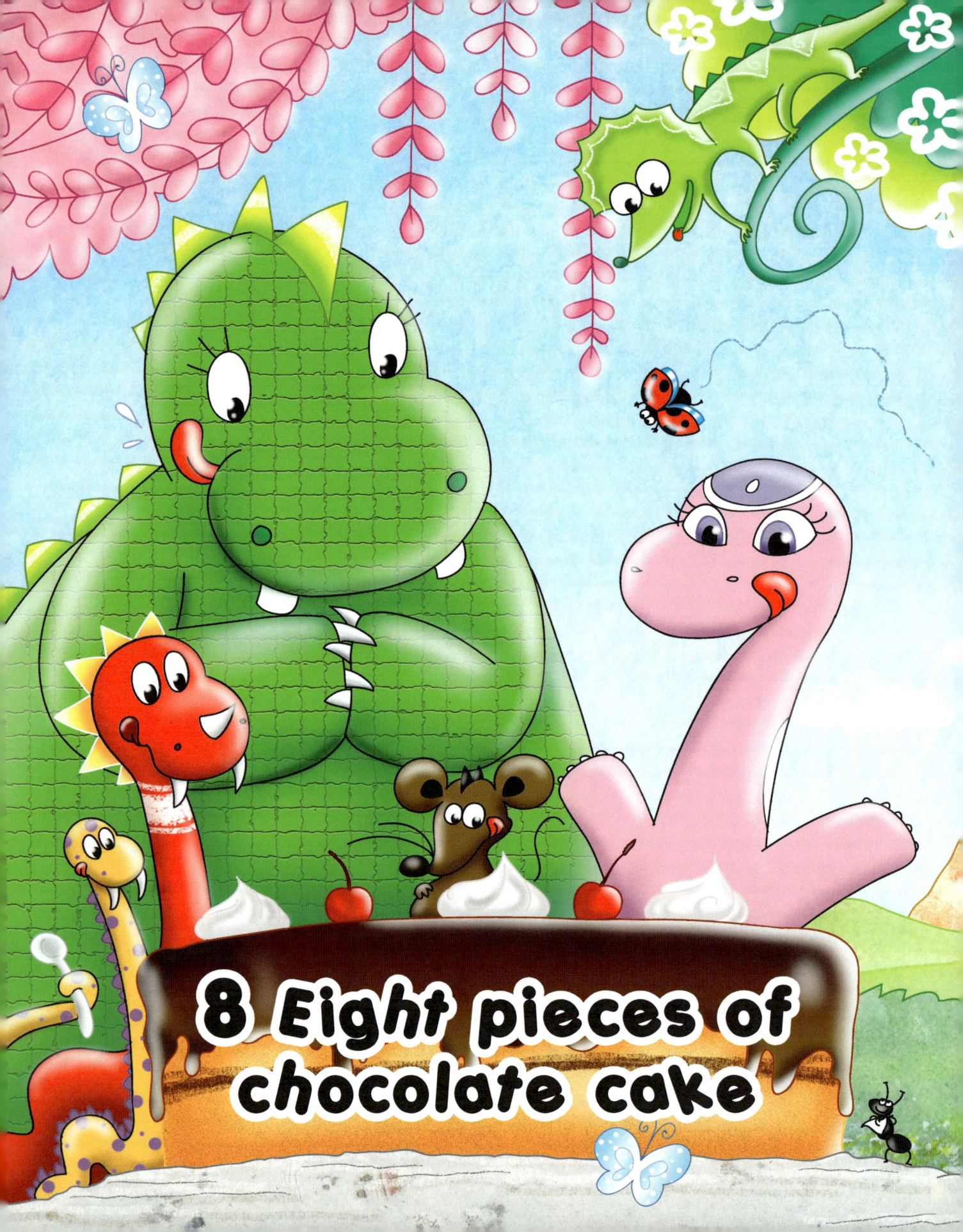

Made in the USA
Charleston, SC
31 December 2012